MARVEL

AVENGERS ASSEMBLY

X-CHANGE STUDENTS 101

By Preeti Chhibber

Illustrated by James Lancett

Scholastic Inc.

All rights reserved. Published by Scholastic Inc., *Publishers since 1920*. SCHOLASTIC and associated logos are trademarks and/or registered trademarks of Scholastic Inc.

The publisher does not have any control over and does not assume any responsibility for author or third-party websites or their content.

This book is a work of fiction. Names, characters, places, and incidents are either the product of the author's imagination or are used fictitiously, and any resemblance to actual persons, living or dead, business establishments, events, or locales is entirely coincidental.

ISBN 978-1-338-84567-9

10 9 8 7 6 5 4 3 2 1   22 23 24 25 26
Printed in the U.S.A.   37
First printing 2022

Book design by Cheung Tai

CHAPTER 1

FROM: Miles Morales <mmorales0811@heatmail.com>

TO: Kamala Khan <k-khan2014@heatmail.com>;
     Doreen Green <acornluvr@heatmail.com>;
     Evan Sabahnur <evan_sabahnur@heatmail.com>

FWD: Extended Field Trip to Xavier's School for Gifted Youngsters

WE'RE TAKIN' A TRIP! Also how does Principal Danvers ignore every single x-quisite pun opportunity in this email. It hurts my brain.

Miles

FROM: Carol Danvers <cdanvers@avengers-institute.com>

TO: Avengers Institute Exchange Students <exchange-avengers-student-list-serv@avengers-institute.com>

Subject: Extended Field Trip to Xavier's School for Gifted Youngsters

Hello students,

We're very pleased to announce a field trip opportunity for students. A small group of second-years will be heading to Xavier's School for Gifted Youngsters to learn from the X-Men. We've contacted your families with a cover story as well as legitimate contact information should anything unexpected happen.

Please remember that you are representing Avengers Institute and act accordingly. You'll find a packing guide and itinerary attached to this email.

Groups will arrive at staggered times, so please check your itinerary carefully.

Col. Carol Danvers
Principal, Avengers Institute

MILES'S JOURNAL

IT IS SLEEPAWAY CAMP TIME. Kind of! We're back for a new semester at Avengers Institute, but all anyone is talking about is our two-week camp at the X-Mansion.

(You could say we're X-cited. No, I won't be limiting my X-puns for this X-cellent adventure.)

Ganke knows where I'll be—but my parents think I'm going to a highly prestigious, rigorous academic program for exceptional students.

I guess you could change that to "X-ceptional" and it would be mostly true, huh?

I wonder how K's getting out of her house for two weeks—Doreen's parents know about her, uh, night job (Which is wild!! My mom would never let me leave my room again if she knew the kind of stuff we got into—I was in a pocket dimension last semester!), and Evan's actually from Xavier's. Hmmm. We should ask Evan about the coolest hang spots. And if there's even decent pizza in Connecticut (that's where Westchester is, right?).

I wonder who else is coming on this trip—and what we're going to learn?? Beast's class was pretty cool, but I want to see what the other X-Men have to offer. Oh man, if Wolverine is teaching us, I am going to sit in the very front of the class.

This is going to be so cool!!!!!

Now I just have to pack—we're leaving in a few hours, and my bags are e m p t y.

XAVIER'S SCHOOL FOR GIFTED YOUNGSTERS

❑ **One Avengers Institute X-Change uniform**

I knew the X-Men wouldn't let us down!!

❑ **Shower shoes & caddy**

Are the showers . . . communal??
Can I shower with my mask on?
Note to self: Talk to the other Spidey

❑ **Your Avengers Institute communicators**

❑ **Train tickets**

. . . We're not just going to teleport there?
We have to take the Metro-North???

❑ **Laundry detergent**

We have to do <u>laundry</u>?!
Do I need to bring . . . quarters?

MILES'S NOTES

Avengers Institute Exchange Program Itinerary

Trip to Westchester:

10:30 AM: Meet at Grand Central Station at the Big Clock

11:11 AM: Depart for Westchester, NY, on the Metro-North Rail

12:33 PM: Arrive in Westchester, NY— Professor Kate Pryde will be waiting for the students to bring them to Xavier's School

1:00 PM: X-change student orientation

1:30 PM: Schedules and dorm assignments distributed

2:00 PM—Evening: Free time

MILES: Hey, man! What should I know about the X-dudes?

THE OTHER SPIDER-MAN: Who?

MILES: The X-Men!

THE OTHER SPIDER-MAN: OH, oh man, I should have understood that. Am I out of touch? Am I . . . old?

MILES: . . . 😊

THE OTHER SPIDER-MAN: Ouch.

MILES: JOKES!

MILES: But anyway, about those X-Men?

THE OTHER SPIDER-MAN: Right, yeah, okay. I taught a class there once, and I think my biggest piece of advice would be do not fly the X-Jet without supervision. It's way harder than it looks. Also, don't borrow money from Wolverine.

MILES: Bro.

THE OTHER SPIDER-MAN: . . . Let me get back to you with something more helpful after I'm done with this Vulture fight.

MILES: You're fighting the Vulture right now???

THE OTHER SPIDER-MAN: I'm multitasking! Also don't text people while fighting. Do as I say, not as I do!

THE OTHER SPIDER-MAN:

THE OTHER-SPIDER MAN: Oops, accidental photo. Ignore it. I'll text later!

CHAPTER 2

What time are we meeting at Grand Central tomorrow? Ten?

Yeah! Then we'll have time to pick up snacks before we get on the train.

Like CINNAMON ROLLS!

AWESOME!

I'm guessing? But come on, we got through a decathlon and a science fair. There's gonna be something!

Spidey's probably right—Evan, spill all the details!

NOD

I don't know too much. I left for the Institute before I really started training, but I'll share what I can.

I have one really important question: Is there good pizza in Westchester?

Uh-oh.

TITLE: X-MEN SCHOOL GUESSING GAME

DOREEN'S GUESS: Nightcrawler! He's blue and furry and has a tail, and also I really wish I could teleport!

KAMALA: Actually that would be *so cool*.

EVAN: Ermmmm, I don't think he's at the school right now, though.

MILES: How do you guys keep track of everyone? There are eight million X-Men.

KAMALA'S GUESS: Wolverine SNIKTTTTT SNIKTTTTT
He is literally unbreakable. Literally.

MILES: I second this. Mostly because I really need it to happen.

EVAN: He's pretty scary, but one time he gave me a dollar so I could get a soda.

KAMALA: WOLVERINE GAVE YOU A DOLLAR AND YOU DIDN'T FRAME IT?!

EVAN: I was really thirsty!!

MILES'S GUESS: It was going to be Wolverine, but I *guess* I'll go with DOOP. *He's* just . . . the weirdest dude I could think of.

DOREEN: Aw, he's cute!

KAMALA: . . . If you say so, D.

EVAN: Uhhhhhhh, let's hope this doesn't happen. Doop's . . . intense. I think if I guess I might be cheating, by the way.

KAMALA: You gotta!!

MILES: You know the most!!

DOREEN: Tell us the secrets, Evan!

EVAN: Ha ha ha ok ok. My guess: Beast and Kate Pryde for sure, and maybe Iceman if he's back from the West Coast? Professor X might even teach us something??

MILES: What else should we get ready for? . . . Like, are we going to know what we're doing?? I don't want to embarrass myself in front of WOLVERINE.

KAMALA: Yeah, seriously. The X-Men are like . . . the X-Men.

EVAN: I really wasn't there for very long! But we've got this!

DOREEN: Yeah! Remember, we just took down a super villain all by ourselves. Maybe you forgot so here's a picture I drew of him. 😁

MILES: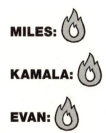

KAMALA: 🔥

EVAN: 🔥

FROM: Charles Xavier <profx@xaviersschool.edu>

TO: Avengers Institute Exchange Students <exchange-avengers-student-list-serv@avengers-institute.com>

Subject: Welcome, Avengers Institute

Hello students,

My name is Charles Xavier, and I am the headmaster here at Xavier's School for Gifted Youngsters. I am pleased to welcome this first group of exchange students to our school, and I have high hopes for how we can all work together. You will be the first of a select group of visiting students. Teamwork is at the core of what we do, and a good team can mean the difference between success and failure.

During your time here, you'll be challenged in new and unique ways, but I fully expect every one of you will rise to the occasion.

Attached you'll find room assignments. Please do not hesitate to reach out with any questions you may have.

Best,

Professor Charles Xavier
Headmaster
Xavier's School for Gifted Youngsters

ROOM NUMBR	NAME
211	Kid Apocalypse
210	America Chavez
207	Ms. Marvel
211	Nova
208	Reptil
208	Spider-Man
207	Squirrel Girl
210	Wasp

CHAPTER 3

MILES: does anyone know who Reptil is????

KAMALA: Oh, I had a class with him last semester—his name's Humberto Lopez, I think? Pretty quiet guy. Kind of a loner?

MILES: I wonder if Nova would switch with me . . .

EVAN: Ask him!!

DOREEN: I think Humberto's nice! Maybe he'll be a new friend. 😄

MILES: You think everyone is nice, D. lolllllll

MILES: I'm gonna look him up online.

Results:

INSTAPHOTO: R3ptil
instaphoto.com/r3ptil

Reptil – Moomblr.com
Snek.moomblr.com

SNEK.MOOMBLR.COM

R3PTIL'S MOOMBLR

these posts are locked

REQUEST TO FOLLOW

REPTIL'S JOURNAL

I can't believe I'm stuck here on this annoying extended field trip. Abuelo never should have made me come. Just because some random lady—fine, even if it's Carol Danvers, <u>Who cares</u>? —says I should go to a super hero school?

"Dear Mr. Lopez" blah blah blah blah blah.

What if I don't <u>Want</u> to be a super hero? What if I just want to be at home?

Plus, I overheard my roommate, Spider-Man, talking to his team on the train and they were all making fun of dinosaurs? Dinosaurs are one of the few cool things in the world! What do they know.

MILES: So . . . Reptil's not the friendliest guy. He ran by me without saying anything, and now I don't know if I'm supposed to wait for him or not?

KAMALA: Oh no, I'm sorry.

DOREEN: Maybe he didn't see you!

EVAN: I asked Nova if he'd swap, but he said we're not allowed. 🙁 But keep trying. Maybe D's right. He might not have seen you!

MILES: It's fine! If he didn't ask me to wait, I guess I won't. I'll meet you all outside after we get changed so we can get the tour?

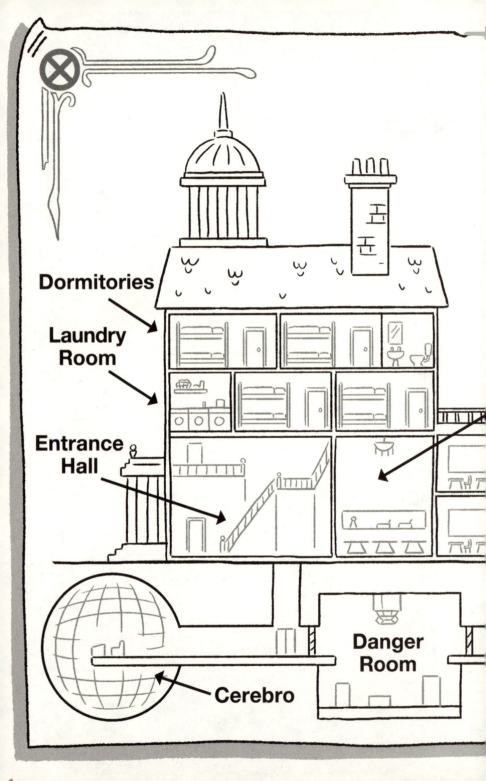

Dormitories

Laundry Room

Entrance Hall

Cerebro

Danger Room

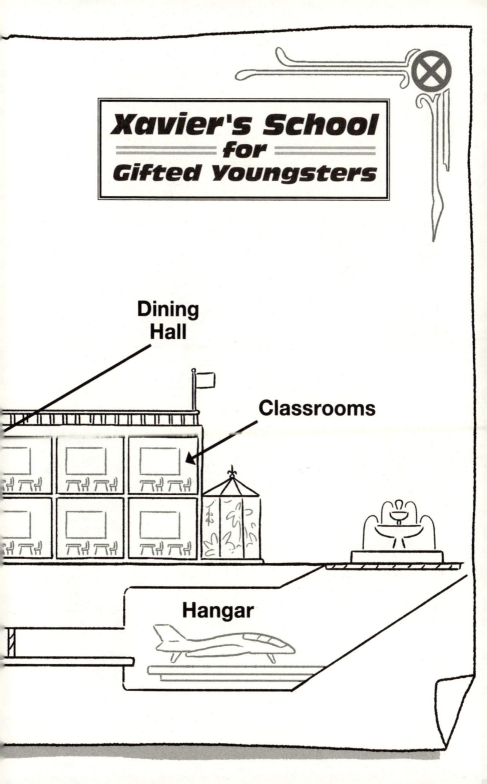

CHAPTER 4

Monday: SUPER HEROING AND YOU 102 with Professor Beast

102??? What are they going to make us do???
Has everyone else taken 101 other classes before this??

Tuesday: TEAM-TEAM-UPS! with Kate Pryde

I wonder what happens when we team-team-team-ups, team^3 ups? Team^infinity ups. Someone put me in charge of naming classes. Also my team wants to be on Wolverine's team.

Wednesday: ACROSS THE BORDER with Wolverine

MY team is going to be on Wolverine's team!!

Thursday: TIME-TRAVEL with visiting professor Bishop

One ticket to the future, please. Heck yeah. But if there are no self-flying cars, I'm going to ask for a refund.

Friday: PLAYIN' THE CARDS WE'RE DEALT, CHÈRE wit' Gambit

I need to ask Spidey about Gambit because I feel like I've heard about some shadiness.

PROFESSOR CARD #242

HANK MCCOY

POWERS

NAME:
Professor
Hank McCoy
AKA Beast

POWERS:
Hyperintelligent, soft and furry, very strong, can hang upside down for long periods of time!

SUPER HEROING AND YOU
(102)

Must ask students what they feel they think they should be learning, how do you become MORE of a super hero?

PROFESSOR: Professor Hank McCoy

OVERVIEW: You're a super hero. Now what?

OBJECTIVE: Young heroes often fall prey to a multitude of issues in their super hero lives once they've become adept at the basics. Problems like hubris, doing things by rote, forgetting to adapt—all issues I've seen happen to the best of us!

NOTES:

- Bring in guest lecturers who have had to contend with issues caused by not thinking (maybe Iceman?).

- DEFs of continuing to learn:

    o Don't forget to think.

    o Evolve constantly, don't get stuck in bad habits.

    o Fight with enemies, not your team!

- What to do when an enemy tries to turn you against one another.

PROFESSOR CARD #077

KATE PRYDE

POWERS

MARVEL

NAME:
Kate Pryde
AKA Shadowcat
AKA Star-Lady
AKA you know what, let's go with Kate

POWERS:
Has pet dragon. Phasing through things, like, SOLID things. And also, through planes of existence???

KATE'S LESSON PLAN

TEAM-TEAM-Ups

Famous examples of team-ups

- X-Men and Avengers of days past
- Be careful about who you bring up.

Questions to answer

- Ideal number of teammates?
- Who is the leader?
- How to decide when no one agrees?

Printouts

- Sample organization charts
- Student questionnaires for pairings

Final essay

- 1,000 words
- What you learned from working with a new team

Group presentation

- 2–4 students
- 5–7 minutes
- Topic: How teamwork saved you
- PowerPoint with 5–10 slides

PROFESSOR CARD #181

WOLVERINE

POWERS

MARVEL

NAME:
Wolverine
AKA Logan
AKA James Howlett
AKA James "Logan" Howlett

POWERS:
Has an Adamantium skeleton, which means he can't break, and very sharp claws that go SNIKT when they come out of his hands. He can heal super-fast. And he's VERY strong.

FROM: Charles Xavier <profx@xaviersschool.edu>

TO: Logan <logan@xaviersschool.edu>

Subject: Lesson Plan?

Logan,

I still haven't received your lesson plans for the Avengers Institute exchange program. As a reminder, you'll be focusing on Canadian super heroing.

Best,

Professor Xavier

FROM: Logan <logan@xavierschool.edu>

TO: Charles Xavier <profx@xaviersschool.edu>

Subject: RE: Lesson Plan?

Puck

Northstar

Sasquatch

Aurora

Snowbird

FROM: Charles Xavier <profx@xaviersschool.edu>

TO: Logan <logan@xaviersschool.edu>

Subject: RE: RE: Lesson Plan?

Logan,

This is just a list of Alpha Flight members.

Please send lesson plan ASAP.

PROFESSOR CARD #311

BISHOP

POWERS

MARVEL

NAME:
Bishop
AKA Lucas
AKA . . . His name is
Lucas Bishop

POWERS:
He can absorb energy, and he has a metal
arm that can shoot nuclear power and that
lets him travel in time. It is VERY cool.

POTENTIAL ERAS TO VISIT - BY BISHOP:

~~Neolithic~~

~~Far Future~~ KANG???

~~Renaissance~~

(Near future)

- Start small
- Need permission slips?

Test past in Savage Land

- Contact current leader (does Savage Land have internet?)

PROFESSOR CARD #266

GAMBIT

POWERS

NAME:
Gambit
AKA Remy LeBeau
AKA The Prince of
Thieves (unconfirmed)

POWERS:
He can use objects to conduct kinetic
energy—usually his trademark playing
cards—and he's a really good thief. But you
shouldn't steal things.

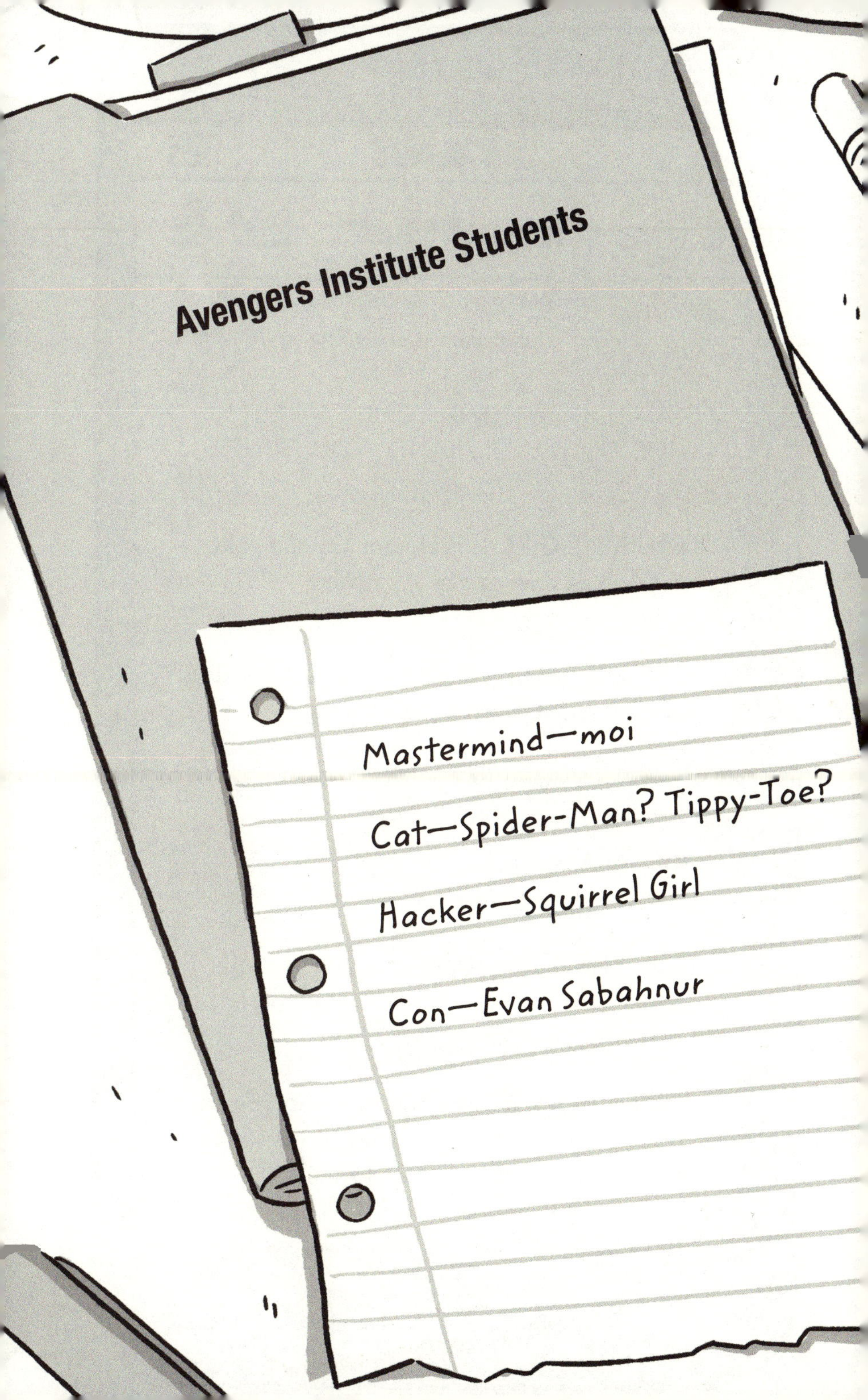

Avengers Institute Students

Mastermind—moi

Cat—Spider-Man? Tippy-Toe?

Hacker—Squirrel Girl

Con—Evan Sabahnur

MILES: These classes are going to be wild.

KAMALA: Time travel!! TIME TRAVEL!! TIME TRAVEL!!!!!!!!!! AND WOLVERINE!!!!

SQUIRREL GIRL: Is Professor Gambit going to teach us how to play . . . poker?

EVAN: No one should bring anything valuable to Professor Gambit's class, agreed?

MILES: Agree

KAMALA: AGREE

SQUIRREL GIRL: Tippy-Toe says "Agree" for both of us.

EVAN: I'm excited to see Professor Beast again—last time he said he was going to tell me his top secret hair mask formula.

KAMALA: You obviously have to share.

EVAN: 😷

KAMALA: Come on!

MILES: Ha ha ha.

MILES: I think the time travel is clearly the most exciting.

SQUIRREL GIRL: I don't know! The team-ups are going to be fun. What if they put us on a team with someone like STORM?

MILES: 😄 Okay, that is a good counterargument!

CHAPTER 5

SPIDER-MAN: Dude!!!

THE OTHER SPIDER-MAN: Who is in charge of the Danger Room while you're in it?

SPIDER-MAN: Kate Pryde?

THE OTHER SPIDER-MAN: Oh, you're fine. Kate's a pro. As long as it's not Gambit or Iceman, you're good.

SPIDER-MAN: You sure? I have serious !!!s about some of these features.

THE OTHER SPIDER-MAN: When have I ever steered you wrong?

SPIDER-MAN:

THE OTHER SPIDER-MAN: Oh, hey, look at the time. I gotta go.

Danger Room Schematics

FIG. 1
SHI'AR COMPUTERS
Four highly effective processing units creating 360 degrees of interactive holographic sequences. Remember to keep the safety on.

How do we confirm safety is on? Ask Professor Pryde ASAP.

FIG. 2
SHI'AR POWER TAPS

Who are the Shi'ar???? Follow up: How come we don't have easy access to alien tech at Avengers Institute? Note to self: Start a petition. Second note to self: Ask Squirrel Girl to start a petition, because she's definitely got a template somewhere.

Originally, the Danger Room was a bunch of blocks and robots, but we eventually integrated alien technology to create extremely realistic holographic training sequences for our students.

FIG. 3
SHI'AR GRAVITIC PROJECTOR ARRAY
& HOLOGRAPHIC TRACTOR AND
PRESSOR BEAM PROJECTORS

So is this the thing that makes it feel like we can actually touch the holograms? Can we make it feel like we are anywhere? Like... a concert? Whose tickets sold out in 3 minutes because of evil bots? And then were reselling online for a million dollars?

Excuse me?

FROM THE DESK OF KATE PRYDE

Avengers Institute X-Change Program
Danger Room—Day One

- Students are excited to be here, though may need to work on some confidence levels

- Will use Program A (lightest & easiest for students new to the Danger Room)

- all kids handled danger room great

- hit program "S" by accident but worked out fine

- slight problem when giant meteor almost fell on one of the kids— looked like un petit dinosaure—but spider-man saved

- med evac was inutile

That was so intense! . . . Evan, are you and Spidey together?

He's hiding out in my room.

Yup.

I can't believe we had to fight holographic *Skrulls*.

Everything felt so real. That was horrible.

I can't believe I saved Reptil's life and he didn't even say thank you.

REPTIL'S JOURNAL

They made us do some serious stuff today, but really, what's the point?

My roommate stopped a huge meteor from falling on me, which was nice, but I felt too weird and didn't say anything to him. He probably thinks I'm a total freak.

And, like, if I wasn't <u>here</u>, I wouldn't have even had to worry about a fake-but-real space rock smashing me to smithereens.

I sent Papa Vic a text message asking to come home, but he just said I need to tough it out. I'm not tough!!

I hate this.

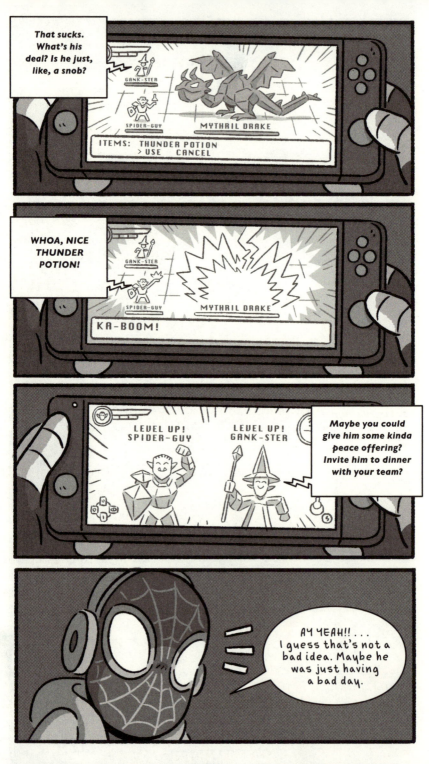

The X-aminer

AVENGERS INSTITUTE X-CHANGE STUDENTS SETTLE IN

WESTCHESTER –In a surprise move from our own headmaster, Professor Charles Xavier, our school opened its doors for students from Avengers Institute, an after-school program for prospective Avengers, led by Colonel Carol Danvers. A surprise because of some past disagreements between the X-Men and the Avengers, but what is the future if not an opportunity for unity! And hopefully not super villains.

We asked some teachers and students what we could expect. Robert Herman (aka Glob) was enthusiastic about the partnership, saying he was looking forward to "meeting new people to hang out with."

Not sure if that constitutes as a burn on the current student population, but we'll leave that up to our dear readers.

Email requests to Professor Iceman were responded to with an auto-reply: NOT HERE, EMAIL WOLVERINE. So we can assume that the subzero professor won't be teaching any of the new students. Professor Logan, on the other hand, had this to say: "Bub, if you don't get outta my face with that phone, it ain't gonna be workin' much longer." Unfortunately, this reporter lost their notes after that interview.

More to come in the next issue of the X-aminer!

The X-amin

Professor Logan (R) cites frustration with our photographer for his burning eggs (L).

CHAPTER 6

FROM: Miles Morales <mmorales0811@heatmail.com>

TO: ad10923@heatmail.com

Subject: hey

Hey Uncle A

two things: I saw your text and heck yeah I want to see that Basquiat exhibit. ill be back home in a few weeks for break. mom already said I can go. (would be down to see the Kehinde Wiley at the Brooklyn Museum, too!) oh, also there's an Edmonia Lewis sculpture being shown at the MET rn—I'm attaching the picture of it. we gotta check it out in person tho.

second, i'm at this camp and my roommate is not interested in hanging— any easy tips on . . . making friends? (don't make fun of me. I know how dorky it sounds.)

miles

ATTACHMENT:

Edmonia.jpg

FROM: ad10923@heatmail.com

TO: Miles Morales <mmorales0811@heatmail.com>

Subject: RE: hey

I'll add the MET to our day of artsing around NYC—and for your camp roommate, just push a little. The kid might be shy or might be going through some stuff. All you gotta do is be kind from your end. You're cool, I mean, you are my nephew ha ha, how could you not be? Little man'll come around.

Uncle A

ADVICE FROM THE OTHER SPIDER-MAN ON HOW TO BE COOL AROUND THE X-MEN, or practical ways to survive Xavier's School for Gifted Youngsters

1. Do not ever look shocked at their powers. Look super chill all the time.

2. The microwave in the second-floor kitchen is way more powerful than a normal microwave. Frozen burritos will only take 5 seconds.

   This isn't really a be-cool tip so much as a live-your-best-life tip

3. Cyclops does not like jokes during battles. Learned that the hard way.

4. Cyclops doesn't really like jokes during not-battles either, unless they're at Wolverine's expense.

5. Do not make fun of Wolverine.

6. Pretend there is a telepath in every room because there probably is.

7. If that telepath is Emma Frost, you are in trouble and should take the first train back to New York. I will pick you up from the station.

and will probably only be an hour late

8. If anyone asks you to play baseball, be on Hank McCoy's team.

9. Oh, bring an extra suit if Nightcrawler's involved because if he teleports you, your suit *will* smell like sulfur.

10. Storm is the coolest person you will meet there. Never forget that.

MILES'S JOURNAL

I've been working really hard to get Reptil out of his shell, but he doesn't want to do ANYTHING.

ME: Oh, cool, what game are you playing?
REPTIL: JUST NEVER ANSWERS?!

ME: Sooo, lunch, am I right?

AND THEN REPTIL JUST LEFT.

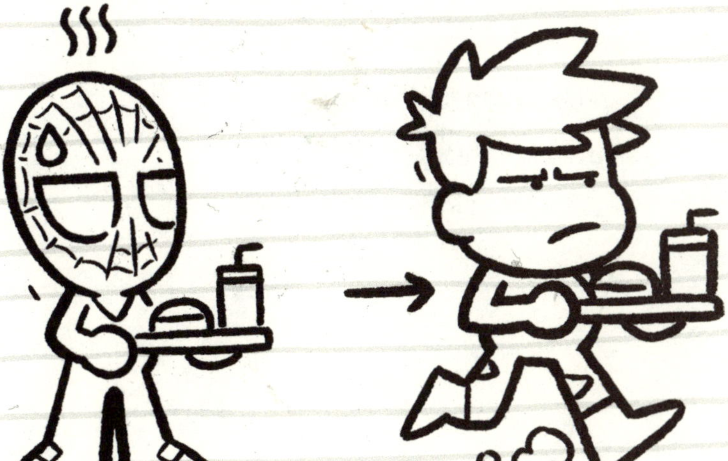

It's all so weird.

Everything else is going great. We had our first class with Professor McCoy today, and he's just as fun as last time. Lots of note-taking, though—could do without so much note-taking. Maybe K will let me borrow her notes.

I'm REALLY looking forward to Wolverine's class, obviously, but I think Bishop's is also going to be exciting. There's a rumor he's going to take us to the Savage Land (though it was Nova who said it, so who knows how accurate that is).

The Savage Land would be so cool—it's like this other planet/dimension where there are ACTUAL dinosaurs! How sweet would that be???

There's so much cool stuff. I wish I didn't have this weird thing happening with Reptil so I could just be enjoying all of it!

HEY, KA-ZAR. WE'RE HOPING TO BRING A CREW OF TWELVE TO FIFTEEN KIDS WITH US, JUST TO SEE HOW THEY CAN HACK A PREHISTORIC-STYLE ADVENTURE. WHAT DO YOU THINK?

THAT SHOULD BE FINE. YESTERDAY I WOULD HAVE HESITATED BECAUSE WE FOUND A STRANGE METAL MACHINE IN THE FOREST, BUT IT WAS QUICKLY DISPATCHED, AND ALL IS WELL.

CHAPTER 7

FAMOUS SUPER HERO TEAM-TEAMS
as told by Professor Katherine Pryde

The X-Men and the Avengers

This one happens a LOT because both of them
have so many members (side note: I need to ask
Spidey if we get cards when we become members or
like . . . a diploma? A certificate?)

But really, there are so many times the X-Men and the Avengers teamed up, and from the way Professor Pryde tells it, it . . . didn't always go well.

Here are some things she says we have to watch out for:

❑ Having two leaders

One time, Thor and Cyclops *both* thought they were leading the team-team and Thor almost broke the *Blackbird*.

❏ Sometimes, there will be members of one team who left the other team, and there is still *drama*. What I will say about that is Vice Principal Maximoff's name came up on more than one occasion.

❏ Wolverine does *not* play well with others. We asked if he could guest lecture and Professor Pryde choked on her water a little bit.

❏ The X-Men . . . really like baseball. Spider-Man was not joking (for once).

REPTIL'S JOURNAL

Here's the thing I don't understand about this school. we have all these classes about teamwork and being a super hero . . . I'm not sure I want to be one at all? It involves so much . . . Relying on other people!

People who I don't even know their real names? How am I supposed to—

It's like . . .

How can I trust people I don't know anything about?

This is so dramatic. Ugh.

My roommate here seems to really like his team. And it seems like his team really likes him. I wonder what that's like. To have friends who really care about you like THAT?

Maybe if I hadn't started so late, if Carol Danvers had found me earlier? If—

Probably not, though. I'm too different.

Anyway . . . With this team stuff, I just don't get it. I only know one thing that's true, and that's whatever is going on in my own head. The only 100 percent certainty there is. I can trust ME.

EVAN: Glob just challenged us to a basketball game, we have to go!

KAMALA: Is this some kind of initiation thing?

DOREEN: I'm in!!

MILES: Obviously this is initiation, so we *have* to beat these x-nerds!

EVAN: You know I'm an x-nerd, right?

MILES: I meant it in the nicest way 😌 😄

EVAN:

KAMALA: I am not good at basketball . . . Unless, powers are allowed????

STARK

TEAM AWESOME

EVAN: Powers ALLOWED

KAMALA: 💪

DOREEN: We're going to have the four of us plus every squirrel in this joint!

EVAN: Okay but powers allowed for everyone else, too, so . . .

MILES: We better hope it's all Glob's level bc I am not playing against a grown-up x-man!!

KAMALA: Oh hey, do you want to invite Reptil? Maybe he likes basketball?

MILES: Nah, he made it pretty clear he's not interested in being friends. 🙍

We can definitely win this. I know there are *basically* two Wolverines out there. But we can do this.

Honey Badger

X-23

Eye-Boy

Glob

FWEEEET!

ᔑᓍᒷ ᔑᓍᒷ ᔑᓍᒷ ᒲᓍᓍᔑᓍᔑᒷ ᕼ ᔑᓍᒷ ᔑᑑᑑᓍ ᓍᔑ ᒲᓍᑑᑑᓍ ᓍᔑᓍ ᕼ ᒲᓍᔑ ᓍᔑ ᒷᕼᓍᕼᓍᒷ ᒲᓍᓍᔑᓍᔑᒷ ᔑᒲᓍᓍᑑ ᓍᔑ ᓍᔑᓍ ᑑᓍᕼᓍᓍᔑᕼ ᒷᓍᓍᔑ *

Umm . . .

It'll be fine! Let's go!

* I'm gonna referee, but I'm also going to film you all. Hope that's cool, because I'm doing it no matter what.

84

* It's what I do. Oh, hey, Evan.

88

I really thought you all were only allowed to play baseball.

What?

I dunno, I was just led to believe there would be way more baseball at this school.

Oh, maybe if it was in, like, the *1980s*.

CHAPTER 8

MILES'S NOTES

TIME TRAVEL

Professor Bishop
Spider-Man

- WHAT IS TIME TRAVEL?
  o Some think: just hop in the time stream and go wherever, but this is wrong
  o Time travel is a highly volatile means of moving through periods on a linear scale of time
  o Pros: We can save people who otherwise might not have been saved!
  o Cons: Time is not structured or safe, must be careful not to make too many changes

o There are *MULTIPLE* futures (WHAT????),
  so always be conscious of when and which
  future you're trying to get to (HOW????)
o B/c there are multiple timelines, we don't
  have to worry about paradoxes (which is a
  HUGE relief, let me tell you)
  • But we DO have to worry about how
    many futures there are and getting lost
    (okay, cool cool cool cool cool)
  • Apparently there are a billion different
    timelines, so no pressure lol *SOB*
o Note to self: ask Spidey about time travel and
  if he's done it and what it's like

- GOALS FOR THE X-CHANGE PROGRAM
  o Create a comfortable affinity for time travel
    among Avengers students (that's us!)
  o Learn about the various ups and downs of
    time travel (seems like there are a lot, so
    maybe I should get a bigger notebook...)

- DIFFERENT WAYS TO TIME-TRAVEL

- o Machines (like Bishop has that machine thing that lets him do it)
- o Magic—someone call Doctor Strange, stat.
- o Super powers—how many X-Men can just…time-travel whenever they want, omg
  - Kind of wish I'd been bit by a radioactive time-traveling spider, not gonna lie.

WE ARE GOING ON A FIELD TRIP

- THE SAVAGE LAND
  - Why not just call it "prehistoric land" or "dinosaur land" or name it after that movie, you know the one? Savage Land sounds brutal as heck.
  - Not actually in the past—the Savage Land is in Antarctica (???)
    - Prehistoric animals do roam the region
      - Dinosaurs

      - Wooly mammoths and saber-toothed tigers????
  - Even though it's in Antarctica, it's tropical
    - Someone in science needs to explain this to me
      - Note to self: email Moon Girl or Amadeus Cho

o There are people who live there, and I
   need to know how they live without the
   internet
o Of course there are also bad guys who live
   there. Of course. Because why not? So,
   super villains we should be aware of:
   • SAURON
      o Is this the Savage Land or
         Middle-earth???
      o Hyper Intelligence, Power
         Absorption, Flight, FIRE BREATH,
         AND HYPNOSIS????
   • STEGRON
      o Super strength, super speed, super
         reflexes, very big and scary tail and
         claws, and can control dinosaurs so
         the Savage Land is probably a good
         place for him to live
- HOMEWORK:
   • Read up on weaknesses for both Sauron
      and Stegron before we leave for the
      Savage Land

Transcript of X-Change Communicators

Logged by Professor Pryde

Parties involved: Gambit

Students:
Spider-Man
Squirrel Girl
Evan Sabahnur
Ms. Marvel
Honey Badger
Eye-Boy

START: ELEVEN HUNDRED HOURS

GAMBIT: Okay, y'all hear me? Tell Gambit if he is too soft; he will change dat up.

STUDENTS, TOGETHER: Roger.

GAMBIT: Now, what we doin' here is a teaching experiment. Y'all will sneak into dis apartment and take back a box I left behind, dat's all. Okay, amis?

EVAN: Um, Professor, should we have . . . signed the *Blackbird* out or anything? Do we need approval for this?

GAMBIT: As dey say back home in N'awlins, Evan, *laissez le bon temps rouler.* Remember what I told you!

SPIDER-MAN: . . . So you want me to get inside of an air duct? This feels . . . wrong.

MS. MARVEL: Professor Gambit, did you get approval from Professor Xavier for this? Should we go—

GAMBIT: Evan, knock on dat door now!

EVAN [muffled]: Hello, yes, my name is Eric Wright, and I'm here to talk to you about supporting your local animal shelter.

[Unidentified voice heard via EVAN's communicator]: What? I don't—I don't have time for—

EVAN: Sir, it will just be a few minutes, and you'll really be helping out with my extra credit.

SQUIRREL GIRL: OKAY, security is neutralized. Spidey, you're a go!

SPIDER-MAN: Well, I guess we are doing this, and I guess I'm going in through this air duct even though, I want to say again, this feels really wrong on multiple levels!

GAMBIT: You all get As if we get through dis, how about dat?

MS. MARVEL: I would not be mad at an A—Honey Badger and I are—

HONEY BADGER: RIGHT HERE IF YOU NEED US.

[Unidentified voice heard via EVAN's communicator]: What was that? Did you hear that?

EVAN: What? OH, I did pass by, uh . . . uh . . . a fight on the way in here. It was messy.

SPIDER-MAN: Okay, I'm in the room. There is a *lot* of stuff in here . . .

GAMBIT: The green box, *mon étudiant*! The green box!

SPIDER-MAN: GOT IT! AH, okay, oops. I hit a column and—

[Unidentified voice heard via EVAN's communicator]: That's my ALARM!

GAMBIT: Okay, I'm coming in. Never fear, Gambit is here!

MS. MARVEL: SIR, WAI—

END OF TRANSMISSION

NOTES FROM PROFESSOR KATE PRYDE:

PROFESSOR GAMBIT TOOK CHILDREN ON AN UNAPPROVED FIELD TRIP TO THE LAIR OF ONE ARCADE. HE THEN EMPLOYED THEM AS PIECES OF A HEIST UNDER FALSE PRETENSES. STUDENTS ARE OKAY. GAMBIT WAS FORCED TO GIVE THE MINI SUPER COMPUTER DRIVE HE STOLE TO THE PROVINCES OF PROFESSOR XAVIER. GAMBIT FOUND A WAY TO APPEASE XAVIER. IT IS MY RECOMMENDATION THAT GAMBIT BE REMOVED FROM TEACHING IMMEDIATELY.

FROM: Kate Pryde <kpryde@xaviersschool.edu>

TO: Avengers Institute Exchange Students <exchange-avengers-student-list-serv@avengers-institute.com>

CC: Carol Danvers <cdanvers@avengers-institute.com>

Subject: Faculty Change

Hello students,

Moving forward, "Playing the Cards You're Dealt" will be taught by Professor Robert "Iceman" Drake. Please update your notes and syllabi accordingly.

Best,

Professor Pryde

FROM THE DESK OF ~~KATE PRYDE~~ Remy

Kitty! Merci for letting me off the hook with these lessons. I'll be back in a few months. Have a job on the other side of the world to handle. Tell the good professor thank you for keeping my equipment safe, but I've got it back with me now, so he don't need to trouble his head about it.

Au revoir!

Remy

CHAPTER 9

Liked by GANKEd and 54 others

Spidey2 Late for this field trip and forgot to do the reading, but I'm sure @Slothbaby handled it, so we're FINE.

Liked by GANKEd and 89 others

Spidey2 Okay, I'm late, but dónde están mis BORICUAS? AQUÍ

THE SAVAGE LAND FIELD TRIP

DURATION: 2 DAYS

CHAPERONES:

BISHOP

WOLVERINE

STUDENTS, GROUPED BY TEAM

TEAM ONE:

signatures

Ms. Marvel _____

Spider-Man _____

Reptil _____

TEAM TWO:

Squirrel Girl _____

Glob _____

America Chavez _____

TEAM THREE:

Evan Sabahnur _____

Nova _____

Eye-Boy _____

TEAM FOUR:

X-23 _____

Wasp _____

Anole _____

TEAM AWESOME

MILES: Did Bishop say we're going for two days but then we're going to time-travel back to this exact point so it will be like we didn't miss any time at all?

KAMALA: That is EXACTLY what he said.

MILES: ;aslkfdnasf

MILES: also i can't believe we're on a team with Reptil

MILES: he hates me

DOREEN: I'm sure he doesn't hate u!!

EVAN: bro no one hates u

MILES: ha ha i mean scorpion doesn't love me that's for sure

KAMALA: super villains don't cfaount lololol

KAMALA: count****

KAMALA: It's gonna be fun—maybe this time we can have dino pets

DOREEN: DINO PETS!!!

DOREEN: Tippy-Toe says she is skeptical

EVAN: At least we'll get some quality time w wolverine lollll

KAMALA:

DOREEN:

MILES:

Okay, so we're not too far from the coordinates they gave us. I wonder what we have to do!

We are DEFINITELY going to fight something big. Get ready to embiggen, Ms. M.

AHHHH, EMBIGGENED JUST IN TIME! Spidey, you handle the webs from up there!

On it!

MILES'S JOURNAL

So, then we all went after this raptor that ambushed us and just...fought it. I webbed up its jaws, K dropped a gigantic fist on its head, and then Reptil just bent his head and used his triceratops skull thing to battle-ram it into the sky. It was AWESOME.

It was the first time I've seen Reptil be part of the team and it was pretty great. He's a nice guy when he's not being all weird and dismissive.

After we beat the raptor, we found our campsite. We managed to get a fire started, eat dinner, and do a perimeter sweep. Camping is EASY. I do kind of wish there was a real bathroom, though. My costume is a onesie and doing your business in the jungle is no joke.

We sat around the fire for a while wondering what the other teams were up to.

I think America probably punched a hole back to Brooklyn.

K brought up that Nadia in her wasp form would fit in super well here. She could find almost anywhere to hide away forever if she wanted to.

Reptil said he bet Nova definitely ate all his rations for the trip in the first half hour. It was funny. But then he kind of looked like he'd shocked himself by speaking up. Then got all quiet again and went to bed.

What is his deal????

MILES: Hey Spidey, I'M IN THE SAVAGE LAND

Message not delivered

MILES: Ugh I think service is bad, let's try this again after I swing up to a tree HEY I AM IN THE SAVAGE LAND AND ON A BIG TREE TRYING TO GET SERVICE

Message not delivered

MILES: Okay fine, you'll get all these messages when I get service again, but we fought a real-life velociraptor today. And that kid Reptil can turn parts of his body into any dinosaur he wants.

Message not delivered

Encrypted text message

This is an automated message. Mutant barrier triggered. *Blackbird* seen entering airspace at 0900 hours. Several mutant beings on board. Engage Operation Take Them All?

CHAPTER 10

MILES'S JOURNAL

This is WILD. We got to the clearing, and everything was just gone. Bishop, Wolverine, the *Blackbird*? All gone.

Our communicators stopped working, too.

I wish I could talk to Ganke—I mean, it's great that K is here, and Reptil has been super helpful, too. But Ganke always knows what question to ask, or what detail I missed. I've sent him a ton of texts, but none of them have gone through.

Being able to get in touch with the other Spidey would also be helpful.

We were talking through what to do and K remembered Bishop saying something about the Savage Land having scientific research bases. She thinks we should head toward one.

"If we can find one of those, we can find a way to communicate with the rest of the X-Men and the Avengers Institute, I bet. Or maybe we can find another way to get out of the Savage Land."

Reptil disagreed. It was awkward because while his point made sense, he was pretty rude about it.

"We don't even know where we are, so how are we going to find a research facility? Sorry, do you have super-science senses now?" he said.

K just looked at him like she felt sorry for him. And then, well—

K did what K does best. Problem solved.

123

CHAPTER 11

REPTIL'S JOURNAL

We're on day three of being stuck in the Savage Land—we haven't seen any of the other teams or any people at all. It's really weird. It also doesn't seem like we're any closer to the research base. Almost like we're going in circles?

Ms. Marvel tries to embiggen and check our progress every few hours, but the pterodactyls are no joke. She can only get up there for a few minutes at a time before they attack. On the ground, it's easier to walk quietly and hide. We've won a few fights with some of the smaller beasts, and I guess we're LUCKY that we haven't seen any other . . . I don't know, organized fighters? The Savage Land is HUGE. I think the longer we're here on our own, the more potential there is for us to get in real trouble.

Not that being stuck in a prehistoric land with no contact with the outside world isn't Real Trouble . . .

One good thing: It's kind of nice being around Spider-Man and Ms. Marvel. I can tell they're not just being fake nice to me. They're being real nice. I feel like I'm an important member of their team. I saved Spider-Man yesterday! Me!

I wish I could tell Abuelo what's happening. I think he'd be happy.

It's still hard—I can't help thinking what if during the next battle they leave me behind. What if I can't help them?? I wish my brain wouldn't think those things, but I try to think about the good things, too.

MILES'S NOTES

MEMORIES OF THE SAVAGE LAND

so I don't forget what I want to post when I get back to having the internet

Luckily Reptil's been great at helping us stay FED. Those rations did not last long enough. The first thing I'm doing when we get home is eating an entire pizza from Sal's. One whole pizza. For me. Not sharing.

Got a timer shot of this one because I HAD to! Major academic decathlon memories 😁

We found this on our second day. It's definitely emitting some kind of signal. None of us are big engineering heads, though, so we just picked it up and brought it with us in case we could use it later. Not sure for what, but you never know!

I am VERY happy that I'm not doing this on my own.

Had to sneak away and wash the suit. It was getting RANK. Spidey's advice was for real. I gotta get a second and third suit, at least.

Ran across this thing in the morning, and my spider-sense went HAYWIRE. Got near it, and it zapped me, like it was trying to  keep something out. Ms. Marvel thinks it means that we're headed in the right direction, and me and Reptil agree. So now we can look out for these little bars, because if they're keeping something out, we probably want to get in.

 WE FOUND IT. Now we have to sneak in. Who knows who owns this place.

CHAPTER 12

MILES'S JOURNAL

That was HORRIBLE. We were fighting Sauron—the WEAKEST name, dude, by the way—when he hypnotized Reptil or something???

Reptil went completely catatonic. K and I were yelling at him to wake up, but nothing! It was so scary. Sauron kept yelling back at us while we were fighting.

"You'll never get me little heroes!" And then MAYBE I webbed his big beak up.

Reptil still hadn't moved, so I was standing in front of him shaking his shoulders.

"REPTIL, we need your help! Wake up!!"

Then Sauron let out this horrifying screech, and all of a sudden we were completely surrounded by drones with lasers. And a huge stegosaurus man. So, if you're keeping score, that's me, Ms. Marvel, Glob, a completely catatonic Reptil against 15 laser drones, a whiny pterodactyl, and a giant stegosaurus man.

Then Sauron got free from my web and started talking again (UGGGH).

"Get them, Stegron, I cannot believe the mutants sent babies to deal with me. Absurd! Come fight me, try to beat my strength, you silly babies!"

Seriously, that's how he talked. He called us "silly babies."

"Ms. Marvel, you handle the big lizard and I'll take the puny one!" I shouted at K, and then totally tornadoed around Sauron. It was the COOLEST thing I have done in a long time.

The drones were responding to his voice, so as long as he was quiet, it gave me a minute to try and get through to Reptil.

"Reptil, come on! You can't listen to this guy. We're still here, fighting! Remember when we beaned that T. rex yesterday? And how you totally saved my life? That's what teammates do. Come on!"

He started to shake a little bit, so I kept going with one eye behind me. Sauron was starting to cut through the web!

"What about when we first got here and were joking about all the other teams—you're a funny dude. I think we can use some more jokes during this fight, man. Let's do this!"

Then he started shaking all over, and I was seriously nervous that I broke something.

AND THEN HE JUST WOKE UP AND STARTED WHALING ON THE DRONES. It was AMAZING.

I did have to stop him for a second, though, ha ha.

"Get Glob!! He's in the most danger!!"

"On it, Spidey!!"

So, Reptil managed to get Glob away, and then it REALLY went down.

143

Kids, handle the drones! Logan and I will deal with these relics.
NO! I WILL HAVE YOUR LIFE FORCE, MUTANT.
Yer welcome to try, but hope you're ready to become dinosaur skewers.
That was a better burn than I expected. I heard Wolverine's not funny.

XAVIER'S SCHOOL FOR GIFTED YOUNGSTERS

MISSION LOG: THE SAVAGE LAND
PROFESSOR BISHOP

STATUS: SUCCESS

Brought four teams of students to the Savage Land. After
sending students out for survival training, Wolverine and I
were ambushed by Sauron and his drone army. I managed
to escape but was wounded. Sauron incapacitated
Wolverine through the use of a strong-acting poisonous gas.

Spent two days in recovery, searching for students.

Was aided by Ka-Zar and his people. They refrained from
engaging in full battle per Ka-Zar's judgment, but it was a
fair one. This was not their fight.

Found Wolverine at Sauron's base—he had one foot out
of the door when I got there. We then located Sauron and
Stegron attacking three students: Spider-Man, Ms. Marvel,
and Reptil. Students were handling it admirably, but
Wolverine and I stepped in to finish the fight.

All students were recovered. We went back in time to the point of leaving the school and ended up in the hangar just after our past selves had left.

Mission log end.

NOTES FROM PROFESSOR XAVIER:

Excellent work, Bishop and Logan. Please note that for future trips, the X-Men should send a team to clear out potential rogue villains prior to sending students in training.

CHAPTER 13

MILES:

THE OTHER SPIDER-MAN: Is that STEGRON?

MILES: yeah, you know him??

THE OTHER SPIDER-MAN: I think he's one of mine. Total dork if I remember correctly.

MILES: Yeah, not a lot of personality happening in ol' Stegron.

THE OTHER SPIDER-MAN: Please tell me you mocked Sauron with Lord of the Rings jokes.

MILES: Did you teach me well?

THE OTHER SPIDER-MAN: mmm yes?

MILES: OH YEAH YOU TAUGHT ME WELL.

THE OTHER SPIDER-MAN: How was the rest of it? How'd you like TSL? (You can be honest. I hate it there. No Wi-Fi? Are you kidding me? It's the savage land but it's still past 2002. Come on.)

MILES: RIGHT???? I couldn't post ANYTHING. It's all right, though. Pretty cool fighting dinosaurs and wooly mammoths and stuff.

THE OTHER SPIDER-MAN: Wooly mammoths?? I've been there a hundred times and I have never seen a wooly mammoth. Consider me jealous.

MILES: 😄

I AM SO GLAD YOU ARE ALL OKAY.

Honestly, we didn't even see much action. Eye-Boy was so good at seeing what was coming that we managed to escape before things caught us. The mammoth only got us because he was asleep.

Same here, really. Sauron pretty much ignored us when he kidnapped Glob. But then *we* got lost. It was a mess! Tippy-Toe says she is never going back there.

I just need to remember to bring a Wi-Fi dongle next time we go, but then I'd totally be down for a camping trip. Those little dinosaurs were pretty cute.

The teeny-tiny ones? The cutest.

They were! And I definitely did not try to take one home as a pet.

Transcript of X-Change Communicators

Students:
Spider-Man
Reptil

SPIDER-MAN: Oh, hey, man. I was just packing.

REPTIL: Oh, oh yeah, that's fine. No worries. I'm just gonna lie down.

SPIDER-MAN: . . . Hey, so, I wanted to say thanks for saving me back on the Savage Land. I'm really glad you were on our team.

REPTIL: I—uh, thank you. That's nice of you to say.

SPIDER-MAN: I'm not trying to be nice. Just being honest.

REPTIL: That's ni—I mean, thanks. Thank you.

SPIDER-MAN: Are you . . . okay?

REPTIL: Yeah, I'm fine.

SPIDER-MAN: You sure? That whole trip was pretty overwhelming. I can't wait to get home and hang out with my parents. Can you imagine?

REPTIL: Ha ha, yeah, I guess I'm ready to see my abuelo.

SPIDER-MAN: You live with your abuelo? That's so cool. I see my abuela a lot, but she doesn't live with us.

REPTIL: Well, my parents aren't around. It's just me and my abuelo. And then he made me come to the Institute . . .

SPIDER-MAN: He made you?

REPTIL: I really didn't want to. I have . . . I have a hard time trusting people, I guess. And all that focus on teamwork and being around *strangers*. It was really hard. People don't really stick *around,* in my experience.

SPIDER-MAN: Oh man, I'm sorry. I didn't know . . . You know that we'll always have your back, though, right? You can't fight a talking dinosaur together and not become friends.

REPTIL: That's really cool of you, Spidey.

SPIDER-MAN: Goes both ways, man. You gotta have my back, too! So it's also very cool of *you*, Reptil.

REPTIL'S JOURNAL

I made some friends. That feels so weird to write. But I think Spidey and Ms. Marvel ARE my friends now. Spidey said I should talk to my abuelo about how I'm feeling, and he might be right.

My abuelo told me about some stuff he went through like this and it just sounded really familiar. Maybe I'm not the only person this happens to?

It's comforting, somehow.

Maybe Avengers Institute wasn't a bad idea, after all.

MILES'S JOURNAL

Well, it's almost a wrap! We're heading back to New York City in the morning—which means I can FINALLY get some good food again—not that the food here was bad, but come on. It's New York. I'll definitely miss hanging out with the X-Men. Though I WON'T miss being tongue-tied when I run into someone like, well...

TWO HOURS AGO:

Me: (walking down the hall, minding my own business, thinking about going to the vending machines)

Me: (looks up and sees the actual STORM WALKING TOWARD ME.)

Me: Hey, Storm! I'm Spider-Man! You're the coolest person here.

Storm: LAUGHS

(I MADE STORM LAUGH!)

Also, I forgot, but after we got back to the hangar when we TIME-TRAVELED, Wolverine told me, K, and Reptil that we "did all right," which, according to the other Spider-Man, is a really big compliment coming from him.

Anyway, this whole thing has been a blast. I hope we get to team up again soon. And I made a new actual friend.

Reptil and I had a good talk. I guess you can't really tell what's going on in another person's life unless you ask them. He said sorry for being a jerk to me in the beginning (even though he really wasn't being a jerk. He thought that I didn't want to talk to HIM, so he thought he was doing me a favor. Can you believe that?), and I apologized for making assumptions.

He's a good guy. I told him we'd have to hang out next semester at the Institute. He's not sure he'll be back after talking to his abuelo, but we exchanged email addresses, so I'm not worried.

Overall: I rate this X-Change an X-CELLENT ADVENTURE.

CHAPTER 14

FROM: Carol Danvers <cdanvers@avengers-institute.com>

TO: Avengers Institute Exchange Students <exchange-avengers-student-list-serv@avengers-institute.com>

Subject: Xavier's School for Gifted Youngsters—Thank you

Hello students,

I want to say how proud I am of all of you for the exemplary work you completed during your stay at Xavier's School for Gifted Youngsters. Professor Xavier was incredibly impressed with all of you. We've decided to turn this into a yearly event, so there will be more field trips in your future! Thank you for being such thoughtful, hardworking students. You did Avengers Institute proud.

I'm also attaching a note from Professor Xavier for you. He wanted to reach out to you personally and share his thoughts.

Col. Carol Danvers

Principal, Avengers Institute

Professor Xavier for Students.pdf

XAVIER'S SCHOOL FOR GIFTED YOUNGSTERS

Xavier's School for Gifted Youngsters
1407 Graymalkin Lane
Salem Center, New York

Dear Avengers Institute Students,

I wanted to share a hearty thank-you for joining us over the last few weeks. The school thoroughly enjoyed having you attend, even for a short time. I would expect nothing less from students of the Avengers. Thank you for being a part of our inaugural program. Next time we'll send some of our X-Men to your hallways.

Best,

Professor Charles Xavier

Avengers Institute Exchange Program Itinerary

Trip to NYC:

10:30 AM: Meet in Xavier School lobby

11:00 AM: Depart for train station

11:17 AM: Depart for Grand Central Station on Metro-North Rail

12:39 PM: Arrive at Grand Central Station

AVENGERS **I**NSTITUTE

KAMALA: I cannot believe we accidentally ended up in the quiet car again.

MILES: How are we so bad at this?

EVAN: I think this was Squirrel Girl's fault.

DOREEN: Tippy-Toe got here first!

KAMALA: DOREEN TIPPY-TOE JUST JUMPED ON SOME GUY'S HEAD, YOU BETTER GET HER

MILES: omg my stomach's going to explode from holding in my laughter, look at that dude's toupee go, Tippy-Toe is using it like a flying carpet.

EVAN: I got a picture I got a picture I got a picture I am crying I got a picture.

KAMALA: LOLOLOLOLOLOL

MILES: I'm making that my phone bg hahahahahaha

DOREEN: OKAY THAT WAS A LOT BUT WE'RE ALL FINE NOW

KAMALA: Hey Miles, did Reptil wanna sit with us? I meant to ask earlier.

MILES: He said he wanted to do some thinking and that he might actually call his grandpa.

DOREEN: That's nice. My grandpa doesn't know how to use his cell phone so we can only call him when he's physically at home.

EVAN: lol wat

KAMALA: ANY way—can we play a game? High and low—tell me the best and the worst thing that happened during the trip. I call dibs on going last.

MILES: lol this is ur idea

KAMALA: yeah so i make the rules lol

MILES: Okay high note? Wolverine telling us we did all right. Also I made Storm laugh.

EVAN: Oh did you make Storm laugh, I didn't know. Did you guys know?

KAMALA: he might've mentioned it once or twice

DOREEN: Or five hundred times

MILES: You're all just jealous bc Storm's the coolest x-man (x-men? x-person?)

KAMALA: ok you're not wrong

DOREEN: My high point was the heist, that security system was so intense and I totally hacked it. I hacked it so fast.

EVAN: I heard that Professor Gambit stole the thing we stole for him from Professor Xavier and they sent Rogue after him.

KAMALA: I BET THEY'RE GONNA KISS

MILES: Ew, they're grown-ups.

KAMALA: It's romantic!!!

MILES: What's your high point, E & K??

EVAN: Mine was getting to show you guys around the school! I kind of grew up there sort of.

KAMALA: Ok, mine was ALSO the Wolverine thing. How many heroes do we have to meet for it not to be the biggest deal of all time?

MILES: I think . . . a lot. Spider-Man told me that when he met Captain America he forgot his own name.

KAMALA: Oh no.

MILES: That's what I said.

STARK

X-23:
Logan

X-23:
Logan answer your phone

X-23:
LOGAN ANSWER YOUR PHONE

WOLVERINE:
what is it, kid
I'm on the road
not a lot of service

X-23:
Are you in the Canadian wilderness again?

X-23:
. . . seeing as I'm literally your clone and can think like you think… gonna assume yes

X-23:
Anyway, when you get enough service, please call—apparently, my time in the Savage Land was a big success and Professor Pryde wants to add me to a team roster, but I need advice—should I join Iceman's?

WOLVERINE:
. . . I'll be back in four hours, don't let her assign you a team before then

OUR X-CELLENT X-CHANGE WITH THE X-MEN

(my attempt at a classic Doreen epic scrapbook)

FROM: Reed Richards <rrichards@futurefoundation.com>

TO: Carol Danvers <cdanvers@avengers-institute.com>

Subject: Avengers Institute Students?

Carol,

Hope things are well. I had the great fortune of seeing Professor Xavier at an event the other night, and he mentioned wonderful things about the work you and Maximoff are doing with these kids at the Institute. Managing to survive a super villain in the Savage Land without help from their chaperones? Impressive stuff.

Can you tell me more about Spider-Man, Ms. Marvel, Squirrel Girl, and Evan Sabahnur?

I understand they're one of your quad-teams. For example, how does this Spider-Man differ from our peer? (I hope he's better at keeping the jokes to a minimum, ha!)

It seems to me there may be an opportunity here for another exchange program—perhaps I can send Franklin and a few of ours over to you.

Let me know what you think.

And please tell Scott I said hello, and that no, I do not have the "super mega battery thing" he's looking for.

Cheers,

Reed

FROM: Carol Danvers <cdanvers@avengers-institute.com>

TO: Reed Richards <rrichards@futurefoundation.com>

Subject: RE: Avengers Institute Students?

Reed—let's set up a call to discuss this week. This sounds great!

Have passed message on to Scott—he'll . . . also be calling you. (Sorry.)

Best,

Carol

PREETI CHHIBBER has written for SYFY, Book Riot, Book Riot Comics, The Nerds of Color, and The Mary Sue. She has work in the anthology *A Thousand Beginnings and Endings*, a collection of retellings of fairy tales and myths, and is the author of the *Spider-Man: Far from Home* tie-in *Peter and Ned's Ultimate Travel Journal* for Marvel. She hosts the podcasts *Desi Geek Girls* and *Strong Female Characters* (SYFY Wire) and has appeared on several panels at New York Comic Con, San Diego Comic-Con, and on-screen on the SYFY Network.

JAMES LANCETT is a London-based illustrator, director, and yellow sock lover! As a child growing up in Cardiff, Wales, he was obsessed with cartoons, video games, and all things fantasy. As he grew up and became a lot more beardy, these inspirations held strong and so he moved to London to study illustration and animation at Kingston University. This degree opened the door to a job he had dreamed of ever since he was a kid, and he now works as an illustrator and animation director.